UNICORN ACADEMY

Freya gasped. A cloaked figure on a tall unicorn with a golden mane and tail was trotting away across the grounds. "Honey!" she yelled, turning to look at the group of unicorns cantering toward them from the stables. "HURRY!"

★ ★ ★

LOOK OUT FOR MORE ADVENTURES AT

UNICORN ACADEMY

★ ★ ★

UNICORN ACADEMY

Freya and Honey

JULIE SYKES

illustrated by LUCY TRUMAN

A STEPPING STONE BOOK™

Random House 🏠 New York

Text copyright © 2019 by Julie Sykes and Linda Chapman
Cover art and interior illustrations copyright © 2019 by Lucy Truman

All rights reserved. Published in the United States by Random House Children's Books, a division of Penguin Random House LLC, New York. Originally published in paperback in the United Kingdom by Nosy Crow Ltd, London, in 2019.

Random House and the colophon are registered trademarks and A Stepping Stone Book and the colophon are trademarks of Penguin Random House LLC.

Visit us on the Web! rhcbooks.com

Educators and librarians, for a variety of teaching tools, visit us at RHTeachersLibrarians.com

Library of Congress Cataloging-in-Publication Data is available upon request.
ISBN 978-0-593-30629-1 (pbk.) — ISBN 978-0-593-30630-7 (lib. bdg.) — ISBN 978-0-593-30631-4 (ebook)

Printed in the United States of America
10 9 8 7 6 5 4 3 2
First American Edition

For Paula Ward

CHAPTER 1

"Come on, Honey!" cried Freya as Honey, her unicorn, weaved in and out of a row of upright poles. Circling around the final pole, Honey raced toward a table with two beanbags on it and a large hoop on the ground. Freya could hear her friends from Diamond dorm cheering them on.

"Go, Freya! Go, Honey!"

"You're in the lead! We can win!"

"Miss the hoop!" chanted the boys from Topaz dorm as Honey skidded to a halt by the table. Freya ignored them. Leaning down and grabbing the first beanbag, she aimed carefully and threw

1

it into the hoop on the ground. Honey nudged the next beanbag closer to Freya's hand with her nose, and Freya threw that one into the hoop too. "Thanks!" she gasped as Honey set off, galloping toward a tall tube standing in the grass.

It was a Sunday afternoon, and Diamond and Topaz dorms were holding an obstacle race at Unicorn Academy. The two dorms got along really well and hung out a lot. They'd set the course up together. The fastest to finish would win, but time was being added on for every mistake each unicorn-and-rider pair made. So far, Honey and Freya hadn't gotten anything wrong!

Reaching the tube, Freya climbed down from Honey's back. She'd been looking forward to this challenge! The tube had a small white ball inside it, and the rider had to somehow get the ball out of the tube without touching it and put it into a cup. There were two long-handled spoons beside

the tube. Everyone else had taken a long time to remove the ball using only the spoons, because they kept dropping it. Freya loved making things work, so this was her kind of challenge.

"I need water!" she told Honey as she dismounted. "Can you get some from the bird bath? As much as you can!"

Not stopping to ask why, Honey galloped to the bird bath, filled her mouth, and galloped back.

Freya pointed to the tube. "In there, Honey!"

Honey spat a stream of water into the tube. As the tube filled up, the ball was pushed upward. When it reached the top, Freya scooped it out with one of the spoons and tossed it into the cup. It had taken almost no time at all.

"We did it!" she cried, jumping onto Honey's back.

The two of them raced across the finish line with Honey's long red-and-gold mane and tail streaming out behind her.

"Freya won!" shouted Rosa, who had been timing Freya's round along with Miki from Topaz dorm. "Diamond dorm is the best!" she whooped.

Freya and Honey were quickly surrounded by the rest of Diamond dorm and their unicorns.

"That was amazing!" said Matilda, throwing her arms around Freya. Freya wriggled away. She didn't really like hugging or being hugged.

"You were so smart on that last challenge," said Ariana.

"I can't believe you thought to use water to get the ball out," Violet agreed.

Freya grinned. "It was fun, wasn't it, Honey?"

Honey whinnied in agreement.

"Rematch!" shouted Himmat from Topaz dorm. "Let's go again."

"Okay," said Rosa. "You're on!"

"Count me out," said Freya. "It's been great, but I've got stuff to do."

"Your big secret invention?" asked Violet.

Freya nodded.

"Oh," Honey complained. "Can't we stay, Freya? Please? You can work on your invention another time."

"No, I really need to work on it now," Freya said, dismounting and giving Honey a pat. "You

can stay, though." Honey didn't know that Freya's secret project was a present for her birthday, which was in just three days. Freya still had a lot of work to do on it.

"It won't be the same without you," Honey said, nudging her with her nose. "Please stay?"

But Freya had to go. She said goodbye and hurried back through the gardens toward the school. Her invention—a robotic unicorn that would bring Honey treats whenever she wanted—had been inspired by the automatic carts that moved hay bales around the stables. It had seemed the perfect way for Freya to combine her engineering skills with showing Honey how much she loved her. She couldn't wait to see Honey's reaction when she saw it!

Maybe she'll be so pleased we'll even bond, thought Freya hopefully. All the students at Unicorn Academy were paired with a unicorn

when they first arrived, and they spent a year at the academy training to be guardians of wonderful Unicorn Island. During that year, the unicorn usually discovered their special magic power and bonded with their rider. Rosa, Ariana, and Matilda in Diamond dorm had already found their unicorns' powers and bonded with them, but Freya and Honey and Violet and Twinkle were still waiting.

Freya hurried toward the school, her mind focused on her invention. When she was near the end of a project, it was like having an itch she couldn't scratch until it was done. There were just a few problems to fix now. The robot was working, but it still wasn't moving properly. *I need to keep it from bumping into things and spinning to the left*, she thought. *But how?*

The buildings of Unicorn Academy looked beautiful in the golden autumn sunlight. The

marble and glass school glittered brightly, but Freya barely noticed. Deep in thought, she headed for the little room next to the art studio that she had been using for her invention. It was time to get to work again!

CHAPTER 2

"Freya!" A banging on the workshop door made Freya jump. She glanced at the clock on the wall. She'd been working on her robot for two hours. The time had flown by!

"FREYA!"

Recognizing Rosa's voice, Freya ran to the door and opened it a crack. "What is it?" she asked.

"Can I come in?" Rosa asked.

"No!" Freya held the door tightly. Seeing Rosa's

frown, she added, "Sorry. I just want to keep this invention secret because it's Honey's birthday present." She didn't want anyone ruining the surprise by accident. Freya squeezed out through the door and shut it behind her. "What's going on?"

"Matilda's had a great idea," Rosa said. "You know everyone at school's been a bit nervous ever since the camping trip?"

Freya nodded. The students had gone on a camping trip in Dingleberry Dell a couple of months ago. It had been really fun until Diamond dorm had discovered that the ancient Heart Tree nearby was being drained of its magic. A cloaked woman had appeared and gone after Matilda and her unicorn, Pearl. They had managed to scare her off, but they still didn't know who the figure was and why she had been draining the Heart Tree. It wasn't the only strange thing that

had happened, either. A few months before that, Diamond dorm discovered that someone had been draining a magic waterfall in the forest. The teachers had no idea who the person was, and all the students were worried. What if they struck again?

"Well, Matilda thought that we should organize a big party to give them something else to think about," said Rosa. "Just students and unicorns, no teachers. We could use the small barn by the stables. It's only got a few bales of hay in it, and no one ever goes there. We're going to have a spooky theme—mix drinks to make a Witch's Brew, make googly eyeballs out of marshmallows, and decorate the barn and stables with fake cobwebs. The boys in Topaz dorm said they'd help. Don't you think it's the best idea ever?"

"It does sound awesome," Freya agreed. "When?"

"On Wednesday night," said Rosa. "In three days."

"But that's Honey's birthday," Freya said.

"Oh." Rosa thought for a second, and then her face lit up with a smile. "Well, it can be a birthday party too! Honey would like that, wouldn't she?"

"Yes, I'm sure she would," said Freya. Honey loved parties and having fun. "I could give her my present at the party."

Rosa high-fived her. "Perfect! And we can all sing 'Happy Birthday' to her at the same time. There's so much to do!" Her eyes shone—she loved planning parties. "We're going to have a meeting after dinner tonight with Topaz dorm. All of Diamond dorm has to be there." She saw Freya make a face. "Nope, no excuses allowed," she said. "You have to be there. Got it?"

Freya sighed. "Got it, Rosa." After having lived with Rosa for ten months, Freya knew there was

12

no point arguing when she was in one of her bossy moods.

Rosa smiled. "Great! This is going to be so much fun!"

After dinner, Diamond dorm met with Topaz dorm to discuss the party. For a second, Freya considered getting away to work on her invention. She was pretty sure she wouldn't be missed. But as she moved toward the door, Ariana caught her eye. "You're not leaving, are you?"

Busted! Swallowing back a sigh, Freya shook her head. "Course not."

Rosa clapped her hands together. "Listen up, everyone. This is a planning meeting for our party. Remember, it's a secret! We don't want the teachers finding out. Okay, let's start with food. What can you all bring?"

"Chocolate!" shouted Himmat.

"Cookies," said Violet. "My nana just sent me a box."

"Hang on. One at a time," ordered Rosa. "Ariana, can you please write a list of food ideas?"

Ariana waved a notebook in the air. "Already on it."

Once the food had been written down, Rosa moved on to the other things they needed to do. Ariana turned the page to start a new list.

"Let's pick some purple pumpkins!" said Matilda. "There are some huge ones in the vegetable garden. We could put them in the barn and have a leapfrog race with them."

"Pumpkin picking," said Ariana, writing it down.

"How about getting some of those giant exploding pea pods?" said Miki. "They're fun. We could play a game to see who can catch the most peas when each pea pod explodes."

"Cool. What else?" asked Rosa.

"Get some apples for apple bobbing!"

"And to make caramel apples with!"

As everyone called out ideas, Freya sneaked a look at the clock above the fireplace. There was an hour until lights-out. She moved toward the door, but as she reached for the handle, Rosa called out, "Where are you going, Freya?"

Freya's heart thumped as all eyes turned her way. "I was just going to work on my invention."

"You're always working on it lately," said Miki curiously. "What is it?"

Rosa snorted. "There's no way she'll tell. You should've seen her face when I tried to go into the workshop this afternoon."

"I'm keeping it secret until Honey's birthday," said Freya. She didn't want to admit that she was hoping it would give her and Honey a chance to bond if it was a perfect surprise.

"Very mysterious," Himmat teased.

Freya rolled her eyes at him and left the room, but as she shut the door she could still hear them talking. She stopped for a moment.

"I wonder why it's such a big secret," said Matilda.

"If we knew what it was, then maybe we could help her," said Violet. "She seems pretty worried about it."

"Maybe we should have a little peek at what she's doing," said Rosa.

Freya's heart started to speed up. No! She didn't want them to! Her friends were the best, but she knew they were all terrible at keeping secrets from their unicorns. It would just take one unicorn to mention something to Honey by accident. Then the whole surprise and Freya's chances of bonding with Honey would be ruined. She ran to the workshop, her mind racing. She needed somewhere safer to work, somewhere her robot wouldn't be found until the party.

She threw her tools into her bag, then put a blanket over the robot and heaved it up in her arms. Leaving the workshop, she glanced left and

right. Making sure there was no one watching, she made her way up the spiral staircase that led to Diamond dorm. She didn't stop at the dorm, though. She kept on going up the tower until she reached a small landing where there was a marble statue of a unicorn's head and a large cupboard in the wall. The cupboard was used for storing old packing crates. *I'll put the robot in here for now,* she thought, *and look for somewhere safer to work on it. There must be a quiet room in the academy I can use.*

The robot was heavy and Freya's arms were aching. With a sigh, she plonked it down, making its wheels clatter loudly on the floor.

"What was that?" She heard Rosa's voice from the bottom of the staircase.

Freya caught her breath. Oh no! The others must be on their way up to the dorm. What if

they came to see what the noise was? Turning the handle, she opened the cupboard and shoved the robot inside. It rolled forward on its wheels and bumped into a wobbly pile of cardboard boxes. The boxes toppled over.

CRASH!

Freya froze in horror.

"There's someone up there!" Freya heard Ariana gasp.

"Let's investigate!" cried Matilda. "Come on, everyone!"

Freya leaped into the cupboard and pulled the door shut behind her. What was she going to do? She leaned against the wall, her heart pounding. Perhaps she could hide behind the boxes. The robot was still hidden under its blanket. There was a chance they might not find her if she was quiet.

Ouch! Something hard stuck into her back. She felt for it with a hand. It was a little lever. Freya pushed it. There was a muffled creak and the wall that Freya was leaning against started to spin slowly like a revolving door. With a startled gasp, Freya fell backward into thin air!

CHAPTER 3

Freya looked around. She was in a secret room! The full moon was shining through the cracked glass of a small window, giving her just enough light to see. The tower room had a dusty desk. There were shelves against the curved walls packed with glass jars filled with old dried herbs. There were a couple of paintings around the room. One was an old picture of a frozen lake, but the picture that caught her eye was a lifelike portrait of a handsome young unicorn with a long golden mane. Stepping closer, Freya saw that the artist had titled the picture "Prancer." She wondered

why it was hidden away in a secret room.

Before she could think about it anymore, she heard the sound of her friends' voices on the other side of the wall in the cupboard. Freya stood still.

"There's no one here." Rosa sounded almost disappointed.

"What was that noise, then?" said Matilda.

"Maybe some boxes fell over," said Violet.

"By themselves?" Rosa asked.

"Well, there's definitely no one up here. Let's go back down to the dorm," said Ariana.

Pressing her ear to the wall, Freya listened as they left the cupboard. She breathed out a sigh of relief. They hadn't found her or the robot. Phew!

As she looked around the room, an idea slowly formed in her mind. This would be a perfect workshop! There was plenty of space to work, and she could get to it really easily from the dorm. Her friends would never find it, and she would be able to finish her robot in peace. Then, after Honey's birthday, she could show the room to the rest of Diamond dorm. A grin spread across her face as she imagined how surprised they would be! A secret room—they would love it! She wished she could tell them all right away, but she only had to wait a few more days.

Going to the revolving wall, she pressed the lever again and spun back into the cupboard. Picking up the robot, she carried it into the secret room. There were some rags on one of the shelves, and she used them to wipe away dust from the desk. As she did, she saw some strange dark scorch marks on its wooden top, as if someone

had placed a burning rope on it. Weird. Freya shrugged. Maybe someone had been doing secret science experiments up here. She turned to her robot again.

Luckily, the unicorn robot seemed okay after being carried around. Freya looked it over. It wasn't very fancy. Built from plain gray metal, it had a rectangular face and funny ears. Its thick neck was connected to a rectangular body, and it held a large basket in its mouth. Its legs were straight and were attached to a platform with wheels. The unicorn didn't have a mane or tail, but

it was still obviously a unicorn. Freya nodded. "Not bad! Now I just need to find out why you sometimes run into obstacles in front of you, and how to stop you from spinning to the left," she said.

It took her a while, but eventually Freya figured out how to change the sensors so that the unicorn would be able to avoid crashing into things. It was voice activated. "Robot . . . forward!" she said.

The unicorn started on a straight path but then turned in a circle. Freya stopped it and tipped it up to look at the motor. Humming softly, she picked up a screwdriver from her tools. She took her time, carefully laying the screws, cogs, and other motor parts beside her on the floor. Everything seemed to be working, and she was sure it was all in the right place. What else might cause the unicorn to turn in a circle? The two axles were definitely the same length. She'd measured them

twice before she cut them. The wheels were the same size, so it couldn't be that, either, unless . . . Freya narrowed her eyes. She'd run out of metal and had to use a new sheet for the last wheel. The metal was a slightly different color, but it looked about the same thickness. She'd been in a rush as usual, though, and she hadn't actually measured it. Removing the wheels, she measured them. One wheel was thinner.

"So that's the problem! If I make all the wheels from the new sheet of metal, they will all be the same thickness."

As Freya pushed her bangs away from her face, she noticed the black greasy stains on her hands. She'd better wash them before bedtime. "Oh no!" she gasped. She'd completely lost track of time. She quickly packed up her tools. She'd leave everything here and come back as soon as she could.

Freya spun back through the revolving wall. She was just stepping out of the cupboard when Matilda came up the stairs. Her face was pale and scared.

"Freya! Phew!" Matilda's breath rushed out with a whoosh. "I heard something moving up here and thought it was a ghost."

"What would you have done if it *had* been a ghost?" asked Freya.

Matilda grinned. "Run to get the others, of course! Anyway, what were you doing?" She frowned. "We heard a noise up here earlier too. Was that you? Why were you in the cupboard?"

"No . . ." Freya started to deny it, but then she gave up. There was no good reason for being in the cupboard, and she knew Matilda would just keep asking questions. "Okay. Busted!" she said, lowering her voice to a whisper. "It was me who made the noise when you all

28

came up earlier. Look, Matilda, if you promise not to tell anyone else, then I'll tell you about something amazing I found."

"I won't," Matilda said. "What is it?"

"It's a secret room with a revolving wall! I'm going to use it as a workshop."

Matilda's eyes grew huge. "Really? That's awesome! Can I see?"

"We'll get into trouble if we're not in bed soon," said Freya, "but I'll show you tomorrow as long as you promise to keep it a secret."

"Okay, I promise!" Matilda said.

CHAPTER 4

"Today, we are starting a new topic," said Ms. Rivers, the strict Geography and Culture teacher. "Open your notebooks and write *Myths and Legends*."

Freya scribbled the words, but her mind wasn't really on the lesson. All morning, Matilda had been shooting secret grins at her. Freya's stomach turned over. She hoped the others wouldn't notice and ask what was going on. Had she made a big mistake telling Matilda? She was a lot of fun, but she wasn't the most reliable or secretive person ever. *I wish*

I hadn't told her, thought Freya, as she neatly underlined the title.

"So, who can tell me any myths or legends that we have here on Unicorn Island?" said Ms. Rivers.

Isla from Ruby dorm put up her hand. "What about the Frozen Lagoon? That's a myth, isn't it? It's a bottomless lagoon that's always covered with ice. It's supposed to be on the east coast of Unicorn Island, but no one's ever found it."

Valentina, also from Ruby dorm, snorted. "Come on. Everyone knows that's just a made-up story."

"Which is exactly why Isla's suggestion is a very good example of a myth, Valentina," said Ms. Rivers sharply. "A myth is a story. It may once have had a bit of truth, but it has been exaggerated and changed over the years. Well done, Isla."

As Ms. Rivers turned away, Valentina made a face at Isla.

Isla quickly looked down at her desk. Valentina was one of the meanest girls at the school, and Freya felt sorry for Isla, Molly, and Ana, who shared Ruby dorm with her. Valentina was in her second year at the academy because she and her unicorn, Golden Briar, hadn't bonded in the first year. Being a second year seemed to make Valentina bossier and ruder each day.

Miki put up his hand. "I know a myth," he said.

"Yes, Miki?"

Freya saw Miki's eyes twinkle. "If you don't graduate from Unicorn

Academy at the end of your second year, you turn into a red-bellied slug with four eyes and a pointed nose. So Valentina had better watch out, hadn't she?" He grinned.

Valentina returned his grin with a death glare.

Ms. Rivers sighed. "No, Miki, you know you don't. Now, does anyone else have a real myth to add?"

Himmat put up his hand. "There's a myth about a ghost who haunts the towers of the academy. It's supposed to be a teacher who once died here. She walks around the halls and climbs the towers at night."

"Is that true?" said Violet.

Himmat nodded. "My brother thought he saw her when he was here."

"Himmat, that's not quite the kind of myth I was thinking about," said Ms. Rivers. "Have any of you heard about the Silver Unicorn? It's

a mysterious unicorn who appears occasionally, always first thing in the morning, and anyone who sees it gets good luck."

Freya made notes as Ms. Rivers continued to tell them about the myths of the land. It was really interesting, and she was surprised when break time came. They all headed to the dining room for cookies and hot chocolate.

"Maybe the noises we heard yesterday from above our dorm were made by the ghost who haunts the school," said Rosa as they left the classroom.

"But ghosts aren't real," Ariana said.

"Well, something made that noise," Rosa told her.

"There could be another reason," said Matilda, sending Freya a look.

Freya tensed. Surely Matilda wasn't going to

give her secret away? "So . . . um, when are we going to tell the other dorms about the party?" she said quickly.

To her relief, her change of subject worked. "We'll tell them now—at break," said Rosa. "Most people will be in the hall, so we can pass the message around. Come on!"

Matilda grabbed Freya's arm and slowed down as Rosa hurried ahead with Ariana and Violet. "Can we see the secret room now?" she whispered.

"Now? But we've got cross-country with Ms. Tulip after break."

"That's half an hour away. We can go to the secret room and get to the stables in time if we leave now."

Freya sighed. "Okay. Let's go. But remember not to tell anyone."

"I won't," said Matilda.

They peeled away from the others and headed for the spiral staircase.

"In here," said Freya, opening the cupboard.

Matilda raised her eyebrows. "But this is just a cupboard."

"No, it's not. Watch!" Freya went to the wall and pulled the lever. There was a familiar creak. She pressed her back to the wall and felt it start to move.

Matilda squealed as the wall revolved and Freya disappeared. Freya pulled the lever again and returned to the cupboard. "So?" she said, her eyes shining.

"Oh. My. Wow!" gasped Matilda, her eyes wide. "What's on the other side?"

"Come and see," said Freya, patting the wall beside her.

Matilda ran to stand with Freya, and Freya pulled the lever again.

"This is so cool!" Matilda walked around the room, slowly taking it all in. "A secret room." She peered at the bottles and jars on the shelves. "It looks like it used to be a science room or something."

"I know. I'm going to use it as my workshop from now on. I'm working on . . ." Freya swept the blanket off her invention. "This! It's a birthday present for Honey," she said as Matilda stared at the robot.

She felt suddenly shy. "What do you think?"

"It's incredible," Matilda said. "Does it actually move?"

"Yes, it's voice activated and can fetch things. It puts that basket down, picks things up in its mouth, drops them in the basket, and then picks the basket up and carries it back. It needs a bit more work because it keeps turning in circles, but I think I know how to fix that glitch." Freya glanced at Matilda. "I know it doesn't look much like a unicorn, but do . . . do you think Honey will like it?"

"I bet she's going to love it!" Matilda exclaimed. "You're so smart! I don't know how you did it." She walked around the robot. "It . . . well . . . it doesn't look very pretty at the moment, though. If you want, I could paint it and give it a mane and tail."

Freya hesitated. She'd never worked on an invention with anyone else, but Matilda was great at art, and she wanted the robot to be as good as possible for Honey. "Yes, please."

"Really?" Matilda clapped her hands. "Awesome! Why don't we sneak away from the others and work on it this evening? I'll bring my paints, and you can bring some cookies or something."

Freya grinned. "Okay, it's a deal!" she said.

CHAPTER 5

Cross-country was one of Freya's favorite lessons—
she loved galloping and jumping, and Honey
loved it too. However, for once she was glad
when their lesson finished. If she was going to
work on the robot that evening, she needed to get
all her homework done during the lunch break.

"Come on, Honey, let's get back to the stables as
quickly as we can," she said.

"Do we have to?" Honey said. "It's a lovely sunny
day. We could go to the playground."

"I can't. I need to do my homework," said Freya.

"There's no time for homework now," said

40

Rosa, overhearing. "We agreed to go pumpkin picking with Miki and Himmat this lunchtime, remember? For the party."

Freya groaned. "Do you really need me? I've got so much to do."

"You have to come and help," said Rosa. "The pumpkins are massive, and it's going to take all of us to pick them and carry them to the stables."

"Okay," sighed Freya.

"As soon as we've settled our unicorns, we'll meet at the stable entrance and go to the pumpkin patch," said Rosa, hurrying away.

Honey snorted. "Do you have to go, Freya? We hardly see each other anymore."

"You see me all the time," Freya said.

"Only in lessons. You never visit me the rest of the time. I miss you."

Freya felt guilty. "I promise that I'll change that

soon," she said. "I'm just really busy working on my invention."

Honey huffed. "I think you like your invention more than you like me."

"I don't!" exclaimed Freya. She wished she could tell Honey that the invention was for her. *It's just a couple more days*, she told herself. *Then Honey will understand.*

"Wow! Look at these pumpkins!" said Freya a little while later as she stared at the sea of massive purple pumpkins in the vegetable garden. She picked her way carefully between the pumpkins, trying not to let their curly green vines trip her.

Miki stopped beside a huge pumpkin. "Someone help me here."

Himmat rushed over and held the pumpkin while Miki cut through its thick, spiky stem. Then Freya and Rosa helped them lift it into

Miki's wheelbarrow. Pumpkin picking took much longer than Freya had expected, but they had a good haul of pumpkins to show for it. They carted them to the stables in the wheelbarrows.

"Goodness me! What are you going to do with all those?" Ms. Willow, the school nurse, came out of her unicorn's stall with some rolls of ribbon in her hands. Everyone really liked her. She was always fussing over her unicorn, Daffodil, decorating her yellow-and-orange mane with fancy braids, or walking around the gardens with her, gathering herbs to make medicines from. Daffodil had healing magic, but Ms. Willow liked to use herbal medicines on sick or injured students whenever possible, so Daffodil wouldn't tire out. She really did adore her unicorn!

"We're going to use them to play a game of leapfrog in the small barn," said Rosa. The others traded secret grins. Rosa had left out that it was going to be a party game!

"In the barn?" Ms. Willow said in surprise. "Why not outside?"

"Just in case it rains," Rosa said. "It's all right if we play in the barn, isn't it? It's never used for anything."

Ms. Willow smiled. "It's fine. Enjoy yourselves!" She headed into the tack room.

Diamond and Topaz dorms wheeled the pumpkins into the old stone barn and arranged

them around the empty space. Their unicorns came out of their stalls to watch.

"They're massive!" said Crystal, Rosa's unicorn.

Rosa nodded. "They're going to be perfect for playing leapfrog." She tried to leapfrog a huge one and got stuck on top of it. She collapsed to the ground, giggling.

Freya suddenly realized Honey hadn't come outside with everyone else. She went to find her. Honey was in her stall, picking at a net of hay. She looked unhappy.

"Are you okay?" Freya said. "Don't you want to come and see the pumpkins we collected?"

Honey looked at her sadly. "Freya, we'll never bond if you keep secrets from me."

Freya stood very still. "Secrets? What do you mean?"

"I overheard Matilda telling Pearl that she's working on a top-secret project with you, and only the two of you know what it is. If you were going to tell anyone about it, Freya, it should have been me."

Freya's cheeks turned red. She should *never* have trusted Matilda! "Matilda wasn't supposed to say anything to anyone," she said angrily. "She promised! Did she say what the project was?"

Honey shook her head. "No, she wouldn't give anything away. Pearl tickled her with her tail and Matilda laughed so hard she got hiccups, but she still wouldn't say."

Freya's anger faded slightly. At least Matilda hadn't said what the secret was.

"Will you tell me the secret too?" Honey asked.

Freya hated seeing Honey upset, but she really wanted the present to be an amazing surprise. *Just two more days, and then she'll realize why I kept it secret*, she thought. "I'm sorry," she said. "I can't." She reached out to stroke Honey, but Honey stepped away. "Don't be like that, Honey," Freya said.

Suddenly, a flash of violet lit up the stables. A second later there was a huge bang from the direction of the barn. It was followed by a series of smaller bangs and shrieks. A thin wisp of smoke curled into the stables. Freya's nose wrinkled. Burnt pumpkin with a whiff of sugar! She rushed from Honey's stall. Miki and Himmat were standing in the middle of the barn, looking like they'd fallen into a gloopy purple swamp.

They were covered in pumpkin flesh and flat pale seeds, and the girls were crowding around them.

"Gross!" A lump of goo slid from Himmat's hands and onto his boots.

"Achoo! Achoo!" Miki sneezed. "That's better," he finally gasped. "I had a pumpkin seed stuck up my nose!"

Ms. Willow came running in. "What just happened? Miki, Himmat, are you both okay?"

"The pumpkins exploded!" Miki exclaimed. "Himmat and I were moving them, and suddenly they went bang!"

"Boom!" said Himmat. "Pow! Pumpkin everywhere!"

Ms. Willow looked shocked. "You poor things. The pumpkins must have been rotten, and exploded in the warmth of the barn. Pumpkins are really best kept outside. It was lucky no one was hurt. Go and wash that off, boys. Everyone else, please help clean up."

Freya grabbed a shovel and headed toward the splattered pumpkins. "I don't understand," she said to Ariana, who was nearby. "The pumpkins were fresh from the field, and the insides don't smell rotten."

Ariana frowned. "So, what are you saying?"

49

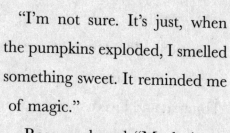

"I'm not sure. It's just, when the pumpkins exploded, I smelled something sweet. It reminded me of magic."

Rosa overheard. "Maybe it was Twinkle or Honey discovering their magic powers."

"What? The power of exploding vegetables?" said Violet, her eyebrows shooting up. "I haven't heard of that before."

Rosa giggled. "Okay, maybe not."

"So, what did make them explode?" said Ariana.

Matilda's eyes widened. "It could have been a spell or an enchantment."

"But who would enchant a load of pumpkins to explode?" said Freya.

"Someone could be trying to ruin the party," said Ariana. "How about Valentina?"

"But her unicorn, Golden Briar, has wind magic, which has nothing to do with exploding things," said Violet. "And Valentina can't cast spells—only people who have a spell-weaver unicorn can do that."

"Also, *why* would Valentina do something like that?" said Rosa. "We invited her to the party at break time, and even though she was a bit snooty about it, she said she'd come. Why would she try to wreck the party?"

"Oh, I don't know," said Ariana. "You're right, it doesn't make sense. Maybe the pumpkins were rotten after all." She sighed and looked around. "I guess we'd better finish up."

CHAPTER 6

"I think I've done it." Freya tightened the last screw and sat back on her heels.

"Let's try it out." Matilda, who had a smudge of paint on her nose, stopped painting.

Freya faced the robot. "Robot . . . on," she said clearly. With a small hum, the robot came to life. "Robot . . . forward," she added.

The robot jerked, then rolled forward, wheeling across the smooth wooden floor. It went in a perfectly straight line toward the enormous blocked-up fireplace, all without spinning or turning. Freya held her breath as it got closer to the fireplace. Was

it going to crash? No! It turned just in time and continued around the room.

"It's working!" Freya said in excitement. "Robot . . . stop!" she said. The robot came to a stop. "I did it!" Freya clapped a hand to her mouth.

"Hooray!" Matilda waved her paintbrush in the air. "You're a genius!" She threw her arms around Freya and hugged her.

Freya stiffened, but Matilda didn't seem to notice. After a second, Freya found herself hugging her back.

"Is all the engineering work done?" asked Matilda. "Can I paint the rest of it now?"

"Yes." Freya stood back and squinted at the robot. "Do you think Honey will like it?"

"She's going to love, love, LOVE it!" exclaimed Matilda. "All the unicorns are going to want one and—"

TAP. TAP. TAP.

A noise came from the fireplace. Matilda and Freya froze.

"What was that?" whispered Matilda.

"I don't know," Freya whispered back.

"Could it be a bird? We had one stuck in our chimney once," Matilda said.

Freya went over to the fireplace and stared at the wooden board blocking it. She realized

something.
"This isn't
just a piece
of wood—
there are
hinges on
one side

and a button on the other. It's a door!" She put her hand on it.

Whoooooooooo! A long drawn-out moan echoed from behind it.

Freya jumped back.

"It's a ghost!" squeaked Matilda. "I bet it's the ghost of the dead teacher that Himmat told us about! Quick, Freya, let's get out of here!" She raced to the revolving wall. Freya darted beside her and pressed the lever. The wall turned and they found themselves in the cupboard. Both of them were breathing hard, and their faces were pale.

"We heard a gh-ghost!" stammered Matilda. "A real ghost!"

But now that she was out of the room, Freya's panic was dying down and her scientist's brain was kicking in. "It can't have been," she said, feeling a bit silly for running away like that. "Ghosts don't exist. It must have been a bird."

"A bird that says *whoooooooo*?" said Matilda. She shook her head. "No. I think it was a ghost and we should tell the others."

"No!" Freya said sharply. "They'll only want to come to the room, and then they'll see the robot. Please, Matilda, don't say anything until after the party—that will also give us a chance to check if we hear anything again. If we tell them it's a ghost and it is just a bird, then we'll look really silly."

"Okay," Matilda agreed after a moment.

They hurried downstairs to the dorm. Rosa, Violet, and Ariana were sitting on the floor

making enormous paper spiders to decorate the barn for the party. With its cozy rug, blue-and-silver blankets, and sparkling fairy lights, the dorm looked wonderfully safe. Freya felt a rush of happiness, until the other three looked up with annoyed expressions.

"Where have you two been?" Rosa asked. "You were supposed to be helping us make decorations tonight."

"Whoops, sorry!" Matilda said. "I completely forgot. I'll help now!" She sat down and quickly picked up some scissors.

"It's not fair for you both to let us do all the work for the party," said Rosa. "There's so much to do."

"I know," said Freya. "And I do want to help. It's just, I've got to finish my invention."

"Because that's more important than anything, isn't it?" said Rosa. "Freya, have you seen how

sad Honey's looking? I guess you didn't, or you'd have been in the stables, spending time with her this evening rather than with your invention."

A guilty blush warmed Freya's cheeks. "Honey understands," she said, pushing down thoughts of Honey's upset face that afternoon. "She knows this is really important to me. As soon as it's done, I'll be able to spend more time with her, so stop being mad at me."

"Rosa didn't mean to upset you—" Violet started to say.

"I did!" Rosa said. "Honey's sad, and we're doing all the work for the party—Freya's being selfish!"

Anger boiled in Freya's stomach. "That's not fair! I—"

A loud crash from the floor above interrupted her.

"What was that?" gasped Ariana.

Matilda's eyes
flew to Freya's, and
Freya knew they
were both thinking
about the noises they'd
heard in the secret room.

Rosa raced to the door,
the argument forgotten.
"Let's find out!"

They ran for the stairs.
Rosa reached the top
floor first. "The statue!" she exclaimed, pointing
at the marble unicorn lying on the floor outside
the cupboard door.

For a moment they all fell silent. "Okay," said
Violet slowly. "How did it fall over all by itself?"

"The same way the boxes in the cupboard just
toppled over all by themselves," said Ariana, her
eyes widening.

"It's a ghost!" squeaked Matilda.

Freya's thoughts raced. The cardboard boxes had been her fault, but what about this? "It can't be a ghost," she said quickly. "Ghosts aren't real." But, even to her ears, her words didn't sound that convincing.

Rosa went to pick it up. "Gosh, it's heavy!"

"Let me help." Freya lifted the statue up with Rosa. As they set it on its pedestal, their eyes met for a second. Freya felt her earlier anger fade away. Of course Rosa had been upset with her. She was worried about Honey and wanted the party to be a success. Freya sighed. "I'm sorry I haven't been helping more, Rosa. I thought you were all having fun planning the party and it didn't matter if I wasn't there."

"We have been having fun," said Rosa. "But it would be even more fun if you were there too."

Freya nodded. "I will be from now on. I promise."

"And what about Honey?" said Rosa.

"I'll spend more time with her and get her present finished too. When she sees it, if she likes it enough, then maybe . . . well, maybe we'll finally bond." Freya struggled to say the last words out loud. She hated talking about her feelings with people, even her friends.

Rosa's face softened. "So that's why you're working so hard on it? Because you think it might help you bond with her?"

Freya nodded.

Rosa sighed. "If I'd known that, I wouldn't have given you such a hard time for not helping out. Sorry, Freya."

"I'm sorry too," Freya said. "And I promise I'll help out more." They smiled at each other.

"I've just thought of something," said Ariana as they headed back to the dorm.

"What?" said Violet.

"Well, if ghosts aren't real, then whoever pushed over the statue and those boxes has to be a person, doesn't it?"

"Like a student or a teacher, you mean?" said Violet.

Ariana bit her lip. "Or the cloaked figure."

They stared at her. "The cloaked figure who was draining magic from the Heart Tree and the waterfall?" said Matilda. "You think she could be here in the school?"

Ariana nodded. "She could be the one who made the pumpkins explode too."

"But why?" asked Freya. "It doesn't make sense. Draining magic from the environment— that's evil. Why would the cloaked figure come

here to knock over statues and make pumpkins explode? It's not the same kind of thing."

"I suppose," said Ariana.

"Freya's right. I bet it's not her. But if she *does* come to the school, she'd better watch out, because we'll catch her!" declared Rosa. "Won't we, Diamond dorm?" She held her hand up.

"Definitely!" everyone chorused, meeting her hand with a group high five.

CHAPTER 7

"Even *more* pumpkins?" Ms. Willow said, looking into the barn with Daffodil, as Diamond **dorm** unloaded a whole bunch of new pumpkins at lunchtime the next day.

"We thought we'd try again," said Rosa. "We really do want to play leapfrog."

Ms. Willow looked at one of the big hay **bales** where they had put a pile of decorations and flashlights. "Hmm. Something tells me that you might have more planned than just a simple **game** of leapfrog, girls." A smile tugged at her **mouth.**

"It's okay," she said. "I won't tell anyone. Your secret's safe with me."

She left the barn with Daffodil. Sighing with relief, Freya and the others began to organize the pumpkins.

Later that afternoon, Freya and Matilda headed up to the secret room. Freya's skin prickled as the wall revolved. Would they hear any strange, spooky noises again? But all was quiet, and she started to relax.

"There!" said Matilda later, standing back and admiring the robot. She had given it a felt mane and tail and painted its body with swirls of color.

"It looks awesome now. Thanks, Matilda," said Freya.

"It's been fun," said Matilda. "This was such a

good idea, Freya. I don't know anyone else who could build a robot."

Freya's heart swelled with pride. Building the robot had been her biggest project so far. She couldn't believe she'd actually done it. And she couldn't wait for Honey to see it the next night. *Oh, please let her love it*, she thought.

She began picking up her tools from the floor. As she did so, her eyes fell on the fireplace. With everything going on, she had completely forgotten about the door in front of the fireplace. She went over to look at it. Yes, there were definitely hinges and an indent that looked like a button on the other side.

"What are you doing?" Matilda asked.

"Just looking." As Freya explored the indent with her fingers, she pressed. There was a click, and the door in the fireplace swung open.

Matilda gasped as a blast of cold air blew into the room. "It's a door!"

Freya peered inside. "And look what's behind it. A tunnel!" A dark tunnel with stone walls and a low ceiling sloped downward.

Matilda joined her. "Where do you think it goes?"

Freya glanced at her. "We could find out."

"But what if we meet a ghost?" said Matilda.

"We won't. Ghosts don't exist," Freya said. A tunnel behind the fireplace explained things. Someone—a person—could have come through it and made noises to scare them. She had no idea *why* someone would do that, but at least it was a reason that she could believe.

She fetched a flashlight from her tool bag. "Are you coming with me?"

Matilda followed Freya through the fireplace and into the stone tunnel. Even with the flashlight, it was hard to see what was ahead of them. They were definitely heading downward, fast. Where were they going to end up?

Freya heard the drip of water. It grew louder as they continued walking, and the floor leveled out. Suddenly, the tunnel opened up into a small chamber. Freya shone the flashlight around. There were two more passageways leading away

from the chamber, and multicolored water was dripping down the walls, forming puddles on the floor.

"I'm guessing the tunnel has brought us out of the school and through the gardens," she said. "I think we're under Sparkle Lake."

"I wonder where those tunnels lead," said Matilda, pointing at the other two passageways.

"Only one way to find out," said Freya with a grin. This was exciting! She headed down the tunnel on the left, which was slightly wider and higher. For a while it went straight, and then it started to slope upward.

"Oh no. It's a dead end," said Matilda as they reached a stone wall.

Freya shone the flashlight on the wall, and they saw some handholds and footholds carved into the stone. Glancing up, she caught her breath. Above them was a trapdoor with light shining around the edges of it. "Look!" She stood on tiptoe and ran her hands over the wooden surface. Finding a small indent, she pressed it. There was a faint click and she felt the trapdoor loosen. She pushed upward and it opened.

Freya pulled herself up the wall using the

handholds and footholds and climbed out. "We're in the barn!"

The trapdoor was hidden in a dark corner of the barn. A layer of straw had been covering it. *I guess that's why we never noticed it*, thought Freya.

"Wow!" Matilda breathed, climbing out. "A secret passageway from our tower all the way to the stables! Isn't this amazing? Just wait until we tell the others!"

"After the party," said Freya quickly. "Or they'll want to explore it and see the secret room. It's perfect! I was wondering how to get my robot out to the barn without anyone seeing. Well, I can use this passageway!"

"Should we go and see Pearl and Honey while we're here?" said Matilda.

Freya stopped to think. Honey had been really

distant with her ever since the day before. "Um, let's not," she said quickly. "We should go back and get ready for dinner before anyone starts looking for us."

"Okay." Matilda grinned at Freya. "A secret room *and* secret tunnels! How amazing is that?"

CHAPTER 8

After dinner, there was a knock on Diamond dorm's door. It was Isla and Molly from Ruby dorm. "We've made some cupcakes," said Isla shyly. She opened the lid of a massive cake pan full of spider cupcakes.

"And caramel apples," added Molly, holding out a plate. "We thought we'd take them to the stables now. Is that okay?"

"Sure, we'll come with you! We can finish putting up the decorations," said Rosa.

They headed down to the barn. On the way, they stopped at the stables to say hello to their unicorns.

All the unicorns trotted out of their stalls to greet their riders—except for Honey.

Freya went into her stall. Honey's nostrils fluttered in a whicker, but then she seemed to stop herself, turning it into an unhappy snort.

"Honey, don't be like this," begged Freya. "Please." She went over and stroked her, but Honey turned away.

Freya's heart twisted in her chest. She knew Honey's feelings had been hurt. She wanted to say she was sorry and tell her how much she loved her, but it was so hard to put her feelings into words. She wished she could be more like Matilda and just blurt out whatever she was thinking.

Instead, she cleared her throat and picked up Honey's water bucket. "I'll get you some more water," she said.

She scrubbed the bucket and refilled it, then put more sky berries in Honey's manger and fluffed up the straw in her bed. "I'll . . . um, see you tomorrow," she said, stopping in the doorway.

Honey gave a small nod. Walking away unhappily, Freya joined the others, who were now decorating. By the time they had finished, the barn looked amazing, covered with fake cobwebs, giant spiders, cut-out ghosts, and cauldrons. There were hay bales to sit on, pumpkins set out for leapfrog racing, a bunch of popping pea pods, and a massive pile of apples on one of the straw bales, ready to be put in a bucket for apple bobbing.

Rosa looked around and gave a happy sigh.

"You know, I really think this is going to be the best party ever!"

Freya didn't sleep very well that night. She kept thinking about Honey and how sad she had looked. She had pictured over and over again the moment when she would pull the blanket off the robot, showing it to Honey in front of everyone. She had imagined Honey's happy face, and a strand of her own blond hair turning red and gold like Honey's mane as they bonded. She really wanted that, but she didn't think she could bear another day of Honey looking so upset. *Maybe I should just forget about the surprise and tell her what I've been doing,* she thought. She tossed and turned and by morning had made a decision. She was going to tell Honey what she'd been doing, even if it meant ruining their chance to bond. She couldn't keep making her unhappy.

Leaving the others asleep in the dorm, she

crept out to the hallway. But as she headed down the staircase, she heard footsteps at the bottom. She froze. It must be a teacher! Moving as silently as she could, she went back up the stairs, past the dorm, and into the secret room.

Letting herself into it, her eyes fell on the robot. An idea formed in her mind. Why didn't she take the robot to Honey now? After all, it was Honey's birthday already. There was no reason she had to wait until the party that evening. *I'll do it*, she thought, feeling a rush of excitement. Tucking the blanket under her arm and getting her flashlight and some rope from the toolbox, she lifted the robot into the tunnel.

"Robot . . . forward!" she said. The robot started to roll down the slope at her side, its wheels clattering on the stone.

When they reached the chamber under the lake, Freya glanced at the passageway on the

right. Where did it lead? If the stables were to the left, then the right must lead in the direction of the vegetable garden. She wanted to find out for sure, but there was no time to explore it. She needed to get to Honey and explain.

A noise came from the tunnel behind her. Freya swung around just as a stone bounced out of it into the chamber.

"Is anyone there?" she asked, stepping forward bravely.

There was no answer. Freya breathed out in relief. The stone must just have been moved by the robot's wheels. "Robot . . . forward!" she said, turning it toward the passageway that led to the barn. The robot rolled on.

It was tricky getting it through the trapdoor at the end, but with the rope, she was able to pull it into the barn. As she climbed out, she thought of an idea. Maybe she could show the robot to

Honey in here and still make it a bit of a surprise! She put the robot in the center of the barn, covered it with the blanket, and headed toward the door. But as she did so, there was a flash of violet light from the direction of the tunnel. She swung around.

POP! POP! POP!

The pea pods that were piled on one of the hay bales started to explode, the peas whizzing through the air. "Ow!" gasped Freya as giant peas hit her. She dodged from side to side as the peas bounced into the opposite wall. What was happening? To her horror, she saw one of the pumpkins swelling. The pile of apples next to the pea pods began to shake, and then an apple suddenly exploded off the pile and shot straight toward her head!

CHAPTER 9

Freya squealed and ducked just in time, but then another apple smashed into her arm, making her yell in pain. She needed to get out of there!

Suddenly, she heard clattering hooves and Honey came bursting into the barn. She ran around the giant pumpkin that was starting to expand and galloped up to Freya. "Freya! I thought I heard you! What's the matter? What's— Ow!" she whinnied as an apple hit her neck.

Honey swung around just as the whole pile of apples exploded into the air. She leaped in front of Freya, batting away the flying apples with her

hooves. She moved so quickly, she was like a blur. Sparks flew up around her, and the smell of burnt sugar filled the air as she swiped apple after apple away. Finally, the last apple hit the wall and Honey stopped. "What's going on, Freya?" she panted.

"I don't know. I—" Freya's eyes widened in horror as she realized the giant purple pumpkin behind Honey was about to burst. "Honey! Watch out! Get behind me!"

Honey leaped toward Freya and swung around.

Freya's mind raced. If the pumpkin exploded in the barn, it would ruin everything—all the decorations and food would be destroyed, and chunks of pumpkin would hit her and Honey. There was only one thing to do. She pulled the blanket off the robot.

"What's that?" gasped Honey.

Freya didn't have time to reply. "Robot . . . on!"

she cried. "Robot . . . forward!" The robot started to roll forward, heading straight for the swelling pumpkin! "Robot . . . faster! Robot . . . DON'T STOP!"

The robot kept moving forward, faster and faster. Freya tensed. Would the voice command keep the sensors from stopping the robot? "Robot . . . keep going!" she yelled.

SMASH! The robot hit the pumpkin at top speed, sending it flying backward. As the pumpkin sailed out the door, it exploded. Purple goo shot into the air and covered the robot. The robot made a chugging, whining noise and stopped moving.

For a moment there was total silence.

"Okay," said Honey. "What's going on?"

"Oh, Honey!" Freya threw her arms around Honey's neck. She held Honey tightly, burying

her face in her soft silky mane. "I'm so glad you're not hurt."

Honey nuzzled her. "I'm glad you're all right too. I heard you scream."

Freya pulled back and looked at her. "You were amazing. The way you swiped all those apples was incredible. How did you move so fast?"

"I think it might be my magic," said Honey.

"Your magic?" Freya gasped.

"Yes, I felt like I could suddenly move so much faster than normal."

Freya blinked. "I did see sparks and smelled sugar. That must have been you! Speed magic! Oh, wow!"

"We can try it out again later and see if I'm right, but first you have to tell me what's going on," said Honey. "Why were you here so early, and what's *that*?" she said, nodding at the sticky purple robot.

Freya quickly explained about the passageway. "I couldn't sleep, so I used it to come here secretly. I wanted to explain why I haven't been spending time with you. The secret invention I've been working on is a present for you." She sighed and walked over to the robot. "Or at least it was. It was a unicorn robot that could bring you treats and things."

"A unicorn robot? For me?" Honey stared at Freya as if she couldn't believe it.

Freya nodded. "I was planning to give it to you at the party. I really wanted it to be the best surprise ever because . . ." She bit her lip. "Well, I thought if I made you really happy, we might bond." Tears pricked her eyes. She quickly blinked them back. She hated crying, but now everything was ruined and she couldn't stop herself.

"Freya." There was a strange note in Honey's voice. Freya looked up at her. "We *have* bonded!"

said Honey. Her eyes sparkled. "Look at your hair!"

Freya glanced down at her hair. On one side there was a bright streak of red and gold. She gasped.

Honey nuzzled her. "I always knew we would."

"What's going on?"

Hearing Rosa's voice, Freya looked around. Her friends from Diamond dorm were approaching the barn on their unicorns. They cantered up.

Matilda gasped. "Your hair, Freya! You've bonded!"

"Yes, and Honey's found her magic!" Freya quickly explained everything, about the invention and her work with Matilda, and what had just happened in the barn, with Honey chipping in. The others' eyes grew wider and wider.

"Speed magic—that's awesome!" said Violet.

"You knew Freya was building a robot, helped her, and didn't tell us?" Ariana said, looking at Matilda.

"It was soooo hard not to. I wanted to, but I promised Freya I wouldn't," said Matilda. "So, who do you think made the pumpkins and peas explode?" she asked Freya.

Freya had already figured out who it might be. "I think it's someone who doesn't want people in this barn."

"But why? No one ever uses it," said Violet.

Freya knew it was time to tell the others the

87

truth. "That's not true. There's a trapdoor at the back of the barn. It leads to a secret passageway that comes out in a chamber under the lake. Another passageway from it leads to a secret room hidden behind the cupboard above our dorm, and there's a third passageway I haven't explored. I think someone wanted us out of the barn so they could use the trapdoor. I think they've also been trying to scare Matilda and me away from the secret room by pretending to be a ghost."

The others gaped.

"This is really serious. We need to tell the teachers that someone's been sneaking around the school," said Ariana.

"Agreed. But before we do that, I absolutely have to see these secret tunnels!" said Rosa.

Freya led the way to the trapdoor. Rosa peered down it.

"You said there's another tunnel you haven't been through yet. Let's explore it and see where it goes!"

"What about us?" asked Honey, looking around at the other unicorns. "We can't get down there with you."

"I think the third tunnel might come out somewhere near the vegetable garden," said Freya. "Why don't you all head in that direction and keep listening for us? We'll call you when we find our way out to the surface."

The unicorns nodded.

The girls dropped through

89

the trapdoor. "Quiet, now!" whispered Freya. "The person who cast a spell on the vegetables might be somewhere around here. I'm sure I heard them following me before."

They carefully made their way along the tunnel. When they reached the chamber under the lake, they paused. "That's the tunnel I haven't explored," said Freya in a low voice.

Rosa pointed to the ground. "Hey, look! Footprints!"

The others joined her. Someone had walked through one of the puddles on the floor and left a trail of footprints leading into the unexplored tunnel.

Matilda crouched. "It's a really strange footprint. The soles of the person's shoes have diamond shapes on them." She pulled out a pencil from behind her ear and the sketch pad

she always carried from her pocket and quickly copied it.

"It must be the person who did the magic and attacked Freya," said Violet.

"Let's follow the trail!" said Rosa.

"Okay, but we need to be even quieter!" hissed Ariana. "The person could be waiting for us."

They headed cautiously along the tunnel. It went straight for a while and then slanted upward.

"Look! There's a light!" whispered Violet.

"I think it's the end of the tunnel," said Freya.

She was right. The tunnel ended in a wall with a gap at one side. They squeezed through it and found themselves standing on damp soil, hidden behind a huge bush. Freya pushed her way around it and stepped out. Where were they?

She saw a brick wall to one side of them and realized it was the wall of the vegetable garden.

They were standing outside the far end of it. Looking to her left, she could see the stables in the distance and the unicorns trotting toward them.

"Honey!" Freya shouted, waving. "Honey! We're over here!" Honey lifted her head and started cantering. The others followed her.

"Freya! Look!" cried Rosa. She was pointing in the other direction. Her voice rose. "It's the cloaked figure!"

Freya gasped. A cloaked figure on a tall unicorn with a golden mane and tail was trotting away across the grounds.

"Honey!" she yelled, turning to look at the group of unicorns cantering toward them from the stables. "HURRY!"

CHAPTER 10

Honey's ears pricked, and gold and purple sparks shot up from her hooves. She leaped forward, and suddenly she was just a blur, leaving the other unicorns far behind. Freya gasped as just a few seconds later Honey arrived beside her. "What is it?" she asked Freya.

Freya was already climbing onto her back. "We have to catch that cloaked figure!" she said, grabbing Honey's mane. "Gallop as fast as you can!"

Whoosh! The noise came from Honey's hooves. More sparks exploded into the air, and the next second Freya felt cold air rushing past her face

so fast it made her eyes tear up. She could feel Honey's muscles bunching and stretching, hear the pounding of her hooves. She realized they had left the others far behind and were catching up to the unknown unicorn.

"Keep going, Honey!" Freya yelled.

They hurried on, getting closer to the figure with every stride. "Stop!" she yelled. "You can't escape from us!" The figure turned and made a flicking motion with one hand. Sparks flew up, and a sheet of thick ice instantly covered the ground behind her unicorn's hooves.

"Honey! Whoa!" Freya yelled. If Honey galloped onto the ice, she would slip and fall. Honey skidded, stopping inches away from where the ice began. Freya almost fell over Honey's head, but managed to hang on to her mane and pull herself down onto Honey's back. She looked up.

"They've gone!" she cried. There was nothing there. The figure, her unicorn, and the ice had all vanished!

Honey gasped for breath.

Freya jumped off her. "Honey, are you all right?"

"Just tired," Honey said. "It was doing all that magic. I'll be okay soon."

Freya hugged her. "You were amazing. Your magic is the best! We went so fast."

Honey whickered. "It was fun, wasn't it?"

Just then, the rest of Diamond dorm came galloping up.

"Where did the figure go?' asked Rosa.

Freya quickly explained what had happened.

"I guess the ice must have just been a glamour—an illusion. We could have kept going."

"You couldn't have known," said Violet. "And you were right not to risk it."

"I wonder how the figure just vanished," said Freya. "One second she and her unicorn were there, and the next they weren't."

Rosa looked around. "I can't see another tunnel or passageway. She may have used magic to disappear. She's done it before, when we saw her in the woods."

The others nodded. "We have to go tell Ms. Nettles about this," said Ariana.

"Then we'll need to clean up the barn," said Rosa.

"I really want to fix the robot before tonight," added Freya.

"I'll help you," offered Matilda.

They went back to the stables. Freya gave

Honey an extra ration of sky berries to help her get her strength back. Then she went to find Ms. Nettles with the others. Ms. Nettles listened seriously, peering down her glasses at the girls as they told her everything.

"Thank you, Diamond dorm," she said when they'd finished explaining. "You certainly have a habit of getting into adventures. I'll look into all this. The cloaked figure appears to know the school very well, which is extremely worrying. We must put some protection spells on these tunnels so that no one can use them to get into the school again. But now"—she raised her eyebrows—"can you please explain to me why you had pumpkins, peas, and apples in the barn?"

Rosa sighed. "We were planning a party. A spooky feast." Ms. Nettles's eyebrows almost hit her hairline. "We're sorry," Rosa rushed on. "Everyone's just been so tense since the camping

97

trip, so we thought it would be good to have something fun to do."

"It was my idea," said Matilda.

"But we were all in on it," said Freya, not wanting Matilda and Rosa to get into trouble on their own.

"Hmmm." Ms. Nettles adjusted her glasses. "Well, maybe this once—just this once—I shall allow the bending of school rules. You may still have your party. But I want you all in bed by ten o'clock at the latest. Agreed?"

They all exchanged happy looks. "Agreed!" they chorused.

The party was so much fun. All the dorms came. There was a lot of laughter, especially when Matilda almost fell into the barrel of water while bobbing for apples. They played Squeak Little Ghost and Find the Spider, shouting out clues

until everyone was hoarse. Honey showed off her new speed magic by whizzing around, catching peas in her mouth as people fired them from exploding pods. Then they sang "Happy Birthday" to her, and Freya, who'd managed to clean up the robot, made it go around the barn with a basket full of caramel apples. Everyone was very impressed as they took one to eat.

"Everyone wants a robot now!" Honey said to Freya happily.

When the games were finally over, Freya sat on top of a massive hay bale with the rest of her dorm, eating plates of delicious food. The unicorns stood around them, tearing off big mouthfuls of the hay.

"So, who do we think the mysterious cloaked figure is?" Rosa asked, waving a spider cupcake. "What does she have against our school?"

"Could it be Ms. Primrose's friend?" Violet asked, licking a caramel apple. "When she was

the head teacher here, someone was helping her do bad things, and they were never caught."

"It might be," said Rosa. "We need to keep a careful watch for anything strange."

"Yes, we're not going to let anyone do anything to the academy. Diamond dorm will stop them!" Freya said.

The rest of Diamond dorm cheered, and the unicorns whinnied.

Honey looked up to Freya. "I love my unicorn robot. Thanks, Freya! This is my best birthday ever."

"For the best unicorn ever." Freya climbed down from the bale and kissed her unicorn's forehead. "I'm sorry I made you sad. I promise nothing will ever come between us again."

Honey softly nuzzled Freya's hair. "Not even a robot?"

"Not even a robot!" Freya grinned.

An adventure across a frozen lagoon
leads Violet, Twinkle, and their friends into
terrible danger. Can they find Twinkle's
magic and save the day?

Read on for a peek at the next book
in the Unicorn Academy series!

Violet and her unicorn, Twinkle, stood very still as the tiger circled them. It looked right at Violet, a growl rumbling in its throat. Violet knew it was only Pearl, Matilda's unicorn, using a glamour—an illusion—but it looked just like a real tiger, and she couldn't hold back her shriek as the tiger pounced. But then she heard Matilda's giggle, and just like that the tiger faded—its paws turning into hooves and its stripy tail growing pink and yellow. Violet grinned as the tiger's last whisker disappeared, leaving Matilda and Pearl in its place.

"Wow! That was great, Matilda! Pearl looked so

fierce. I really thought she was going to eat us," said Violet.

Twinkle nodded, adding, "It was very good, even though I could see bits of Pearl's mane showing through the glamour at the end."

Pearl frowned. Matilda gave her a hug. "Doing a glamour is really hard. It takes a lot of magic to keep it going. I think you were amazing, Pearl."

"Me too," said Violet, shooting a look at Twinkle. She knew he didn't mean to be unkind, but sometimes he just said what he thought without realizing how it might sound. She did love him, but she found his bluntness pretty embarrassing at times. She was the complete opposite of him—she really hated hurting people's feelings.

Nearby, the rest of Diamond dorm were practicing their magic too. Honey, Freya's unicorn, was galloping super fast around the frosty garden.

Crystal, Rosa's unicorn, was making a snow twister dance across the lawn, and Whisper, Ariana's unicorn, was standing under a tree with a family of timid rabbits playing around his hooves.

When the young unicorns and students first arrived at Unicorn Academy, they were put into pairs by the head teacher, Ms. Nettles. The students lived at the academy and attended classes, where they were taught how to care for their unicorns and learned all about their home on beautiful Unicorn Island. They also had to discover their unicorn's magic power and bond with them. While most unicorns and riders could bond in a year, some needed to stay for an extra year.

Violet's hands played with Twinkle's thick blue-and-purple mane. When they finally bonded, a strand of her dark hair would turn the same colors. She bent down and hugged him. "I hope we find your magic soon," she whispered. Violet loved being at the academy, but she didn't want to be the only one of her friends who stayed for another year.

"Don't worry," Twinkle said confidently. "We will. I bet I'll have something much better than Whisper's or Crystal's magic."

"Shh!" Violet hushed him as her friends came riding over.

"I don't know about all of you, but I'm ready for hot chocolate," said Rosa.

"Me too, and the unicorns deserve lots of sky berries," said Matilda.

The unicorns whickered happily. Doing magic used a lot of energy, and sky berries were really good for helping them recover.

Diamond dorm rode across the grounds. It was a frosty winter's day, and the school buildings were framed by the blue sky, the glass-and-marble towers sparkling in the pale sunlight.

"It's so strange to think we won't be here after graduation at the end of December," said Ariana.

"Twinkle and I might still be," said Violet. She

gave her friends a worried look. "You'll all write to me, won't you?"

"No," said Rosa.

Violet's heart sank.

Rosa grinned. "We're not going to write because you're not going to be here. You and Twinkle will discover his magic and bond very soon. We're all going to graduate together. It'll be perfect!"

The others smiled, and Violet felt a little better.

"It would be even more perfect if we could catch the cloaked figure before we graduate," said Freya.

During their year at the academy, the girls in Diamond dorm had come across a mysterious cloaked woman three times. Back in the spring, they had found out that she was taking magic from the Verdant Falls. And in the summer, they had discovered she was draining magic from the ancient Heart Tree. A month ago, she had tried to scare them out of an old barn on the school grounds where they had been planning a secret party. It turned out that the barn hid the entrance to a bunch of hidden tunnels. The mysterious woman had been using the tunnels to move around the school unseen, but no one knew why.

"I'm glad the teachers put protection spells on all the entrances to the tunnels so that only teachers and students can use them now," said Violet. Knowing that had made her feel much safer.

"I just wish we could work out who the cloaked figure is," said Freya.

"We've got lots of clues." Rosa started counting them off on her fingers. "One, she's been gathering magic power. Two, she knows a great deal about the school and its hidden tunnels. Three, her unicorn is tall and fast, has a long golden mane, and can cast glamours."

PuRRmaids

Meet your newest feline friends!

PuRRmaids

The Scaredy Cat

1

Sudipta Bardhan-Quallen

New friends. New adventures.
Find a new series . . . just for you!

For ballerina and fairy and vampire lovers

For adventurers

For unicorn lovers

For dog lovers

For mermaid and cat lovers

For sports fans

Isadora Moon: cover art © Harriet Muncaster. Magic on the Map: cover art © Stevie Lewis. Unicorn Academy: cover art © Lucy Truman. Puppy Pirates: cover art © Liz Tapia. Purrmaids: cover art © Andrew Farley. Purrmaids® is a registered trademark of KIKIDOODLE LLC and is used under license from KIKIDOODLE LLC. Ballpark Mysteries: cover art © Mark Meyers.

1220b

RHCB rhcbooks.com

PUPPY PIRATES

Ahoy, mateys!
The treasure hunt for your next
favorite book ends here!

rhcbooks.com **RHCB**

∼ Collect all the books in the ∼
Horse Diaries series!

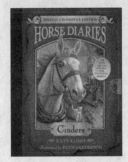

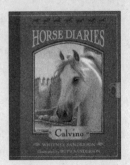

Every Isadora Moon adventure is totally unique!